SCOOBY-DOO! and YOU: THE CASE OF THE BIGFOOT BEAST

A Collect the Clues Mystery

By Tracey West

WORLDWIDE PUBLISHING™

SCHOLASTIC INC.

New York   Toronto   London   Auckland   Sydney
Mexico City   New Delhi   Hong Kong

ISBN 0-439-21751-2

12 11   2 3 4 5/0

Cover and interior illustrations by Duendes del Sur
Cover and interior design by Madalina Stefan

Printed in the U.S.A.

First Scholastic printing, September 2000

"Glad you could make it," Daphne calls to you as you walk into the diner.

Servers carry plates of food to the booths in the busy place. Daphne, Fred, Velma, Shaggy, and Scooby-Doo are seated by the window. You join them.

Velma slides over and makes room for you in the booth. You sit down. Across the table, Shaggy and Scooby are steadily munching on a foot-high stack of pancakes.

"Like, this is so much yummier than that back-to-nature food we've been eating at the campground," Shaggy says. "Nothing but nuts and berries. Right, Scoob?"

Scooby slurps up the pancakes in one

bite. He nods his head. "*Ruts and rerries. Ruck!*" Scooby makes a face.

"We went on a camping trip," Fred explains. "There's nothing like a little fresh air to clear your mind after solving a mystery."

"Of course, we found *another* mystery at the campground," Velma says. "We just can't seem to escape them."

"We didn't just find a mystery. We found a monster, too," Shaggy says, shivering. "Man, that thing was big and hairy!"

Velma looks at you. "We sure could have used your help."

"You like solving mysteries, don't you?" Daphne asks. "We call this mystery *The Case of the Bigfoot Beast*, she says. "Why don't you read our Clue Keeper?" she asks as she hands you a colorful notebook. "You can try and figure out the mystery as you read. I was the writer for this mystery's entries."

"We write down the details of the mystery in the journal," Fred says. "The people we meet. The clues we find. They're all in there."

"We've even made them easy to find," Daphne continues. "When you see these spooky eyes , it means we found a suspect. And a flashlight  means we found a clue."

"At the end of each entry, we'll help you organize the information you've found," Velma added. "All you need is a pen or pencil and your own Clue Keeper notebook."

You take the Clue Keeper, a little nervous. Are you really as clever at solving mysteries as the Scooby Gang?

Fred smiles at you. "Don't worry. I bet you'll crack the case in no time!"

Clue Keeper Entry 1

"Like, are we there yet, Daphne?" Shaggy asked, huffing and puffing. He had a heavy duffel bag on his back.

"Almost, I think, " I answered.

Fred had parked the Mystery Machine in the parking lot of the Happy Camper Campground. Then the gang and I had all grabbed our sleeping bags and backpacks and started hiking up the hill to the campground entrance.

"I think that's the office up there," Fred said. He pointed to a small log cabin at the top of the hill.

A man with a white beard stood in front of the cabin. He was talking to a tall, bald man wearing a suit.

"You're making a big mistake, Walden!" said the bald man. "I'll make you an offer you can't refuse."

He stormed off down the other side of the hill. The bearded man shook his fist.

"I'll never sell!" he cried. "Never!"

"He sure looks like one *un*happy camper to me!" Shaggy remarked.

The man with the white beard noticed us. He smiled and held out his hand.

"Hello, campers!" he said. "I'm Henry Walden. Welcome to the Happy Camper Campground!"

"Is everything okay, Mr. Walden?" Velma asked.

Walden's smile faded. "Oh, you mean my argument with Rick Richardson," he said. "He's the owner of the resort down the hill. For years he's been trying to buy the campground from me so he can expand. But I love this place too much."

"I can see why," said Fred looking at the

surroundings. "Where can we pitch our tents?"

Walden stroked his beard. "We've got lots of campsites open," he said. "Follow me."

Walden headed down a path lined with tall trees. As we walked farther into the woods, the sun disappeared behind the leafy branches.

"These woods are beautiful," I said, but Shaggy and Scooby didn't agree.

"There's something creepy about this campground," Shaggy said.

Mr. Walden stopped. "Why do you say that?" he asked nervously.

Shaggy held out his arm. "Like, I've got goosebumps on my goosebumps," he said. "Everyone knows that woods are filled with spooks and ghouls and stuff."

"I hope you're wrong about that," Mr. Walden said as he continued down the path.

The path led to a clearing.

"I'll help you set up camp here," he said. "It's a nice spot. It's near all the major trails." He pointed to three different trails leading into the woods.

Velma and I set up a small tent. Mr. Walden helped Fred set up another one.

"Shaggy and Scooby, you can sleep in here with me," Fred told them.

Scooby crawled into the tent and poked his head out.

"Hey Scoob," Shaggy said. "Now it's a *pup* tent! Get it?"

"You can unroll your sleeping bags now, guys," Fred said.

Shaggy and Scooby looked at each other.

"*Reeping rags?*" Scooby asked.

"You mean you didn't bring any?" Velma asked. "What's in that heavy bag?"

"Important camping supplies," Shaggy said. He opened his duffel bag.

A tower of food spilled onto the grass. Giant hero sandwiches. Coconut cream pies. Fried chicken. Donuts. Bagels. Corn on the cob.

Shaggy turned to Velma and me. "This is all Scoob and I need to survive in the great outdoors. As long as our stomachs are happy, we'll be happy. Right, Scoob?... Scoob?"

Shaggy turned back. Scooby-Doo was standing in front of the bag, which was now empty. He licked his lips with great satisfaction.

Shaggy grabbed the bag and shook out the crumbs. "Like, this is terrible! We'll starve in these woods without food. We've got to leave right now."

"Please stay," said Mr. Walden. "You're my only campers this weekend."

"I was wondering about that," Velma said. "Why is the campground empty? It's the height of camping season. And why did you get so jumpy when Shaggy said the campground was creepy?"

Mr. Walden looked at his boots. Then he looked back at Velma. "I can't lie to you kids. Campers have been scared away from this place because of a story. A silly story."

"What story?" I asked.

Mr. Walden sighed. "People say the Bigfoot Beast is stalking the campground."

"*Rigfoot Reast!*" Scooby jumped into Shaggy's arms.

"I've never seen it myself," Mr. Walden said. "I assure you, this campground is safe. And I'm right down the road if you need me."

"Don't worry Mr. Walden," Fred said. "We've faced our share of monsters before. We'll be all right."

Mr. Walden nodded and headed back down the trail.

"I'm sure there's nothing to be worried

about," I said. "We're going to have a great weekend, right guys?"

Shaggy and Scooby didn't answer. They were hiding in Fred's tent.

"Like, we'll have a good time as long as that Bigfoot Beast stays far away!" Shaggy replied.

"Did you catch the 👀 on page 5? Fred and I thought you would. That means you've found the first suspect. Answer these questions about this suspect in your Clue Keeper notebook."

1. What is the suspect's name?

2. What kind of work does he do?

3. Why might he want to keep people away from the campground?

11

Clue Keeper Entry 2

It didn't take long for us to set up camp. Velma took a pair of binoculars out of her pack.

"I bet this is a great place for bird watching," she said. "Anybody want to come along?"

"Sounds like fun," I said.

"I think I'll work on getting us some dinner," Fred said.

"*Rinner?*" Scooby licked his lips.

"I think Scoob and I will stay with Fred," Shaggy said hungrily.

Velma nodded. "We'll be back soon."

Velma and I followed a trail. We marched along through the tall, dark trees. Soon the trees began to thin out, and we found ourselves in a clearing on top of the hill. Flat, gray rocks stretched out before us.

We walked onto one of the rocks and looked down at the scene below.

"Gosh," I said, "This sure is a nice view."

"Get off of there right now!" a voice cried.

We both spun around. A tall woman wearing jeans and a blue shirt was glaring at us. She wore a cap on her short, red hair. She carried a pack on her back.

"Those are Archaeotherium tracks you're stepping on!" the woman said angrily.

Velma and I looked down. Under my feet I could see what looked like hoof prints cut into the rock.

"We're sorry," Velma said, jumping off the rock. "The Archaeotherium is a prehistoric animal, right? You must be a paleontologist. A scientist who studies fossils."

"That's right," said the woman. "I'm Mindy Podwick."

Then she eyed Velma suspiciously. "You seem to know something about paleontology. Are you here to steal my discovery? Because I found it first!"

"Of course not," I replied. "We're here on a camping trip."

"We're just out bird-watching," Velma added. "We didn't mean to disturb you. Mr. Walden didn't mention anything about a fossil discovery."

Mindy Podwick's face clouded. "How many times do I have to tell Walden to keep people away from here? It's going to take me weeks to fully uncover these tracks. I'll never get my job done if heavy-footed tourists keep trampling the site."

Velma and I exchanged glances.

"We'll go bird watching somewhere else," Velma said. "Nice to meet you."

Mindy didn't reply. She was busy brushing dust away from the fossil prints.

"That was a little strange," I said as we walked away.

"You can say that again!" Velma agreed.

"Hey, did you spy the 👀 back on page 13? You've found another suspect! Answer these questions in your Clue Keeper notebook."

1. What is the suspect's name?

2. What kind of work does she do?

3 Why might she want to keep people away from the campground?

16

Clue Keeper Entry 3

Back at the campsite, Shaggy and Scooby-Doo each held a fork and knife.

"So Freddy," Shaggy said. "Like, where's that dinner you were talking about?"

"*Rmmm. Rinner!*" Scooby echoed.

"I haven't caught it yet," Fred replied.

Shaggy and Scooby looked at one another, confused.

Fred dug in his pack and took out a pocket fishing pole and a small tackle box.

"One of the reasons we chose this campground is that there's a stream here that's perfect for fishing," Fred said. "If I'm lucky, I can catch us some fresh fish for supper."

"Fresh fish?" Shaggy asked. "Like, do you think there are any pizzas swimming around in that stream?"

Scooby rubbed his tummy. "*Rmmm. Rizza!*"

"I'm pretty sure there are only fish," Fred said. "Do you want to come?"

"Fishing's just not my bag," Shaggy said. "I'd rather get my food from a snack machine."

"Fine with me," Fred said. "But I don't think you'll find any snack machines in these woods!"

Fred took off down a trail. Shaggy and Scooby sat down on a fallen log.

Grrrrrrrrr! A rumbling sound filled the air.

"What was that?" Shaggy asked, alarmed. "Is it the Bigfoot Beast?"

Scooby smiled sheepishly and pointed to his stomach.

"I know how you're feeling, Scoob," Shaggy said. "I'm so hungry I could eat this log."

Just then, a delicious smell wafted into their campsite. Shaggy and Scooby sniffed the air.

"Are you thinking what I'm thinking, Scoob?" Shaggy asked.

Scooby-Doo nodded.

"Let's follow that smell!" Shaggy cried.

Shaggy and Scooby followed their noses down a trail — the same trail Fred had taken. Soon they saw the stream flowing nearby. Then the trail forked to the right.

They followed the delicious smell and took the fork. Just up ahead, a small cave was set into the side of a hill. A man had a campsite set up in front of the cave. He was sitting in an old lawn chair cooking hot dogs over a fire.

"Who's there?" the man called out as he heard Shaggy and Scooby approach.

"Like, we're just some hungry travelers searching for a good meal," Shaggy said.

The man eyed them suspiciously. "How did you find me?" he asked.

"We followed our noses, right Scoob?" Shaggy said.

"*Right!*" Scooby replied.

"If I give you some food, will you leave me alone?" the man asked.

Shaggy and Scooby nodded.

The man pointed to some hot dogs cook-

ing over hot coals. The hot dogs were attached end to end on one long string.

"Help yourself," he said. "Name's Skinny. Skinny Miller. I'm the caretaker of this campground."

Skinny Miller lived up to his name. He was thin, with short, gray hair and piercing blue eyes. He was as tall as Shaggy, but his feet looked small compared to Shaggy's big shoes.

Shaggy picked up one end of the hot dog string. Scooby picked up the other. They chomped on the hot dogs until they met in the middle.

"Fancy meeting you here, Scoob," Shaggy joked. He gulped down the last bite and

looked at Skinny. "So, you're the caretaker. Like, isn't it weird working out here in these spooky woods?"

"This job wouldn't be so bad if that penny-pinching Walden would pay me what I'm worth," Skinny said. "I do all the work around here, and he makes all the profit."

"So, like, why don't you just leave?" Shaggy asked.

Skinny's face clouded. "I could have made a fortune in my family's jewelry business. But my father was a bad businessman. He lost everything. So I'm stuck here. Besides, these woods don't scare me."

"So I guess that story about the Bigfoot Beast is a big lie," Shaggy said.

Skinny looked him right in the eyes.

"Oh no," he said. "I've seen the Bigfoot Beast. He haunts these woods every night!"

Shaggy and Scooby's
Mystery-Solving Tips

"Like, did you see the 👀 on page 21? Groovy. Jot down the answers to these questions in your Clue Keeper notebook while Scooby and I go look for a snack."

1. What is the suspect's name?

2. What kind of work does he do?

3. Does he have a reason to keep people away from the campground?

Clue Keeper Entry 4

Later that night, the gang and I were all sitting around the campfire toasting marshmallows. Fred, Velma, and I each had one marshmallow on a stick. Shaggy and Scooby's sticks were filled with marshmallows from top to bottom.

Shaggy told us how Skinny Miller could have made a fortune in the jewelry business, but he was stuck working at the campground instead. But that's not what worried Shaggy.

"I'm telling you, Skinny said he saw the Bigfoot Beast," Shaggy was saying between bites. "He said it haunts the woods at night."

"I bet he was just teasing you," Velma said. "I'm sure Mr. Walden's right, and the Bigfoot Beast is just a silly story. I wouldn't be surprised if Mindy Podwick made it up. She doesn't want anyone near her fossils."

Shaggy still looked worried. "I don't know. Skinny seemed pretty convincing to me, right, Scoob?"

"*Mmm mmm,*" Scooby replied.

"What's that, Scoob?" Shaggy asked.

Scooby pointed to his mouth. "*Mmm mmm mmm.*"

"I think Scooby's had one marshmallow too many," Velma said. "His mouth is stuck!" She handed Scooby a water bottle.

Scooby took a sip. "*Rat's retter!*" Scooby said.

Feeling tired, I stood up and yawned. "I'm going to get some sleep," I said.

"Me, too," Velma said. She followed me inside our tent.

"You mean we're really going to stay here overnight?" Shaggy asked. "What if the Bigfoot Beast gets us?"

Fred put out the campfire. "Don't worry, guys.

Just get a good night's sleep. I bet you won't even think of the Bigfoot Beast in the morning."

Fred walked into the boys' tent and climbed into his sleeping bag. Shaggy and Scooby rushed in after him. Since they hadn't packed any sleeping bags, they tried to get comfortable on the hard ground.

Fred fell asleep right away. But Shaggy and Scooby tossed and turned. Scooby's tail smacked into Shaggy's face. Shaggy's feet jabbed into Scooby's back.

"Like, this is a hopeless cause," Shaggy said. "We're never going to get to sleep."

Scooby-Doo sighed.

"Hey," Shaggy said. "I bet Mr. Walden has some comfy beds in that log cabin of his. We should go there."

Scooby looked scared. "*Rout rhere?*" He pointed out into the dark night.

Shaggy reached into Fred's pack and

took out a flashlight. "We'll be okay, Scoob. Mr. Walden's cabin is right down the road and besides, I bet there's food in the fridge."

"*Rokay!*" Scooby said.

Shaggy and Scooby stepped out of the tent. Shaggy shone the light on a trail.

"I think it's this way," Shaggy said.

Shaggy and Scooby walked through the dark woods. The flashlight lit the way ahead.

On the side of the trail, two yellow eyes glowed in the darkness.

Scooby jumped into Shaggy's arms.

"Zoinks!" Shaggy cried. "It's the Bigfoot Beast!"

The yellow eyes got closer. Then a little raccoon ran in front of the light.

Scooby jumped down, looking embarrassed.

"Like, it was just a little critter," Shaggy said.

Shaggy and Scooby marched on.

"We should have reached the cabin by now," Shaggy said, a little worried.

The trail opened up into a clearing.

"Man, Scoob, it looks like we took the wrong trail," Shaggy said, chuckling nervously. "We'll have to go back."

Then Shaggy and Scooby noticed another pair of yellow eyes gleaming in the darkness.

"It must be another raccoon," Shaggy said. He called out. "Hey, little fella! Are you looking for your friend?"

The yellow eyes got closer.

"Here, little guy," Shaggy said.

Something jumped in front of the flashlight. But it wasn't a raccoon.

It was a tall creature, taller than Shaggy. The beast was covered with long brown fur.

It had two big, hairy feet.

"Like, it's the Bigfoot Beast — for real!" Shaggy cried.

"*Aaaaaargh!*" The Bigfoot Beast roared and lunged after Shaggy and Scooby.

Shocked, Shaggy dropped the flashlight.

"Run for it, Scoob!" Shaggy yelled.

Shaggy and Scooby tore back down the trail. They ran to the campsite and crashed into Fred's tent.

"Everybody run!" Shaggy yelled. "The Bigfoot Beast is after us!"

Clue Keeper Entry 5

Fred's tent came crashing down. Shaggy and Scooby got tangled up in the fabric. Fred stepped out of the mess.

Velma and I ran out of our tent.

"Jinkies!" Velma cried. "What's going on?"

Shaggy and Scooby tried to get out of the tent. But the fabric covered their eyes. They hopped around, trying to get loose. Then they crashed into our tent. That tent collapsed, too.

Velma pulled the tent off them.

"What's this all about?" Velma asked, yawning.

"Like, there really is a monster in these woods!" Scooby said. "The Bigfoot Beast. We saw him. He chased us down the trail."

Scooby put his paws out in front of him and growled like the beast.

Shaggy explained how he and Scobby had gone out to look for Mr. Walden's cabin when they found the beast in the clearing.

"I believe you," Velma said.

Two flashlights appeared in the darkness. Skinny Miller came down one trail. Mr. Walden came down another.

"My goodness!" Mr. Walden said. "Is everything all right?"

"It is now, Mr. Walden," Fred said. "But a few minutes ago, Shaggy and Scooby saw the Bigfoot Beast!"

"I told you," Skinny said. "He haunts these woods at night. I've seen him. He's got beady eyes as red as rubies."

"That's him all right!" Shaggy said.

Mr. Walden glared at Skinny. Then the worried look returned to his face.

"Are you sure?" Mr. Walden asked. "Maybe it was just a deer."

Shaggy and Scooby shook their hands. "Like, this was a big, hairy, beast! There was nothing *dear* about it."

"This is terrible," Mr. Walden said. "I can't let people camp here if there's a beast running lose. I'll have to close the campground."

"Don't worry, Mr. Walden," Velma said. "We'll help you solve this mystery. If we find out what's behind this beast, you can keep the campground open."

"You kids will really help me?" Mr. Walden asked gratefully.

"Sure," Fred said. "We'll start investigating in the morning."

"I wouldn't go looking for that beast if I were you," Skinny muttered. "It's dangerous."

"We've seen our share of monsters before," Velma told him. "We can handle it."

Mr. Walden looked at the mess in their campsite.

"Why don't you all sleep in my cabin tonight?" he suggested. "I've got extra beds."

"Now why didn't we think of that, eh, Scoob?" said Shaggy.

"Thanks, Mr. Walden," I said. We all followed Mr. Walden to his cabin, and soon we were sound asleep.

In the morning, we all headed back to the campsite. Fred started to pick up the tent poles.

"I'll get this straightened out," Fred said.

"I'll help," I offered.

Velma turned to Shaggy and Scooby. "Why don't you show me where you saw the beast?" she asked.

Shaggy looked around the campsite. There were three trails to choose from.

"Like, I'm not sure which trail we took," Shaggy said. "We ended up in some kind of clearing."

"That sounds like the trail Daphne and I took yesterday," Velma said.

I nodded in agreement.

"Follow me," Velma instructed to Shaggy and Scooby.

Shaggy and Scooby were a little nervous as they walked down the trail. They expected the Bigfoot Beast to crash through the trees at any minute.

Soon the trail opened into a clearing. Mindy Podwick was kneeling on a long, flat rock. She looked upset.

"Did you do this?" she asked Velma. "I told you and your friend to stay away from here!"

"What happened?" Velma asked.

"Somebody's been walking all over my Archaeotherium tracks," she said. "I can tell because there are footprints everywhere."

Velma examined the footprints.

"They're not very big," Velma remarked. She turned to Shaggy and Scooby. "Shaggy, these are too small to be yours. And there are no paw prints, so they can't be Scooby's. They must belong to the Bigfoot Beast."

"Like, for somebody named Bigfoot, he's got really small feet," Shaggy said.

"Good point," Velma said. She turned to Mindy Podwick. "Are you sure they aren't your own footprints?"

"They're about the same size," Mindy Podwick said. "But I would never trample all over my fossils. I know better than that."

She eyed Velma. "What's this about, anyway? Is it that silly beast that Skinny Miller keeps talking about?"

"It sure is," Shaggy said. "That hairy horror attacked us last night."

Mindy Podwick raised an eyebrow. "Really? I thought old Skinny was making it up. I can't say I minded it, though. At least it kept people away from my fossils. Until now."

"Well, we'll leave you alone now," Velma said, taking the hint that Mindy Podwick didn't want them around anymore.

"Okay...bye," Mindy muttered distractedly.

Velma led Shaggy and Scooby back down the trail. Birds chirped in the trees.

"Like, these woods aren't so scary when it's sunny out," Shaggy said. "I can't believe we saw the Bigfoot Beast here last night."

Scooby shivered remembering the events of the night before.

"After seeing those small footprints, I don't think we have too much to worry about," Velma said.

"Did you see the on page 34? That's your first clue. Write down the clue in your Clue Keeper. Then answer these questions:"

1. What clue did you find in this entry?

2. What does this clue tell you about the Bigfoot Beast?

3. Which of the suspects could have left this clue?

Clue Keeper Entry 6

Back at the campsite, Velma told Fred and I about what happened in the clearing.

"It sounds like someone is behind this Bigfoot Beast," Fred said.

"I'd rather be *behind* it than like, in front of it!" Shaggy said. "That's one scary monster."

"Besides Mindy Podwick, who would want to scare people away from the camp?" I asked.

Velma thought. "How about the man Mr. Walden was arguing with yesterday? Mr. Richardson, the resort owner? If Mr. Walden has to close the campground, Richardson could buy it from him."

"Good thinking," Fred said. "I also think we should talk to Skinny Miller. He seems to be the one who's spreading these stories about the Bigfoot Beast. And he doesn't like Mr. Walden much. Maybe he's in on it somehow."

"I'll go with you, Fred," I said.

"Scoob and I will go with Velma," Shaggy said. He rubbed his stomach. "I bet that resort has a five-star restaurant."

Velma, Shaggy, and Scooby-Doo headed to the resort. When they reached the bottom of the hill, a fancy gate opened into a sprawling green lawn. A white mansion lay at the end of the road. Next to it was a sparkling swimming pool.

Velma spotted Mr. Richardson by the pool. They approached him.

"Mr. Richardson, we're staying at Mr. Walden's campground," Velma said. "We were wondering if we could talk to you for a minute."

"Certainly," Mr. Richardson said. He led

them to a round, glass table. "Why don't you join me for a snack?"

"*A Rooby Rack?*" Scooby asked.

"Like, Scoob, I think there'll be some fancy resort food at this place. That's even better than a Scooby Snack," Shaggy said, licking his lips. He sat down and flagged a waiter. "We'll have two of everything on the menu, please."

"Nothing for me, thanks," Velma said. "Mr. Richardson, we were wondering about your interest in Mr. Walden's campground."

"Oh, that," Mr. Richardson said. "That Henry Walden can be so stubborn. I've offered him a great deal of money. He just won't sell. I need that land so I can expand this place."

"Do you want it badly enough to drive Mr. Walden out of business?" Velma asked.

"Goodness, no," Mr. Richardson said. "Henry and I have been friends since we were boys. I'm sure my money will convince him in time."

Mr. Richardson crossed his legs. Velma studied his shiny black shoes.

"Those are nice shoes, Mr. Richardson," Velma said. "Do you mind if I ask what size they are?"

Mr. Richardson laughed. "They're a size sixteen! Big feet run in my family."

Velma stood up. "Come on guys," she told Shaggy and Scooby. "I think we can go now."

The waiter sat a covered silver tray in front of them.

"In a minute, Velma," Shaggy said. "Scooby and I are just about to dig in."

Shaggy lifted the lid. He revealed a plate piled high with carrot sticks, celery sticks, and lettuce.

"Like, what kind of snack is this?" Shaggy asked.

"This is a health resort, young man," Mr. Richardson said. "We only serve raw fruits and vegetables here."

"Thanks, Mr. Richardson," Shaggy said. "But Scoob and I will pass on the rabbit chow."

As they walked back up the hill to the camp, Shaggy's stomach rumbled.

"Maybe we should go see if Skinny has any more hot dogs," Shaggy said. "I'm hungry!"

"*Re roo!*" Scooby agreed.

"I'm anxious to talk to Skinny Miller myself," Velma said. She walked ahead quickly.

Shaggy sank down on a rock. "We'll catch up with you in a minute, Velma," he said. "All this back-to-nature stuff is wearing me out."

Scooby sat down next to Shaggy.

Up ahead, the tree branches rustled.

"Velma, is that you?" Shaggy called out.

"Aaaaaargh!" The Bigfoot Beast crashed through the trees. He waved his hairy arms and stomped his feet.

"Zoinks!" Shaggy cried. He and Scooby tore up the trail at top speed. They crashed into Velma.

"Hang on, guys," Velma said. "What's wrong?"

"B-b-b-b," Shaggy stammered.

"The Bigfoot Beast?" Velma asked.

Scooby nodded.

"Let's check it out," Velma said. She walked back down the hill.

The Bigfoot Beast was nowhere in sight. But Velma saw something glittering on the ground.

She took out her magnifying glass and knelt down. Then she picked up something very tiny. A chip of a shiny blue stone.

"Jinkies," Velma said. "This looks like a sapphire."

"Fire? Where's the fire?" Shaggy asked.

"I said sapphire," Velma said. "It's a valuable gem."

"Way out," Shaggy said. "You mean gems grow on trees in these woods?"

Velma shook her head. "Actually, sapphires are usually found in stream beds or gravel pits."

She stood up.

"We've got to find Daphne and Fred!" she said.

"Did you see the on page 44? Velma found another clue. Man, I wish Scooby and I had a pizza for every clue she's found! While we're dreaming of pizza, you can answer these questions in your Clue Keeper."

1. What clue did you find in this entry?

2. Where on the campground do you think the clue could have come from?

3. Does this clue give a new reason for someone to scare people away from the campground?

Clue Keeper Entry 7

While Velma, Shaggy, and Scooby-Doo hiked back up the hill, Fred and I were looking for Skinny Miller.

We found the stream and the cave next to Skinny's campsite. The campfire was out. His shabby lawn chair was empty. Fred called into the tent, but no one answered.

"I wonder where Mr. Miller is?" I asked. I put my hand on Mr. Miller's chair and noticed something odd.

"Fred, look at this," I said. I picked up a book from the seat of the chair. "It's a directory of gem dealers — people who buy and sell valuable stones. I wonder what Skinny's doing with this?"

"I'm not sure," Fred said. "Shaggy said he used to be in the jewelry business. Maybe he's trying to get back in."

"I wish we could ask him about it," I said.

"We'll have to see if Mr. Walden knows where to find him," Fred replied.

"It's too bad he's not around," I said, walking toward the stream. "It's so pretty here," I said, looking at the water.

I looked closer. "That's strange," I said. "The bottom of the stream bed looks kind of sparkly."

"What are you kids doing here?" an angry voice cried.

Fred and I spun around. Skinny Miller was coming out of the cave with a scowl on his face. His gray hair stuck out on top of his head.

"Sorry, Mr. Miller," Fred said. "We're trying to help Mr. Walden solve this Bigfoot Beast mystery."

"There's no mystery," Miller said. "The beast roams these woods. Just like I told your friends."

"Mr. Walden might have to close this campground," I said. "Then you'd be out of a job."

Mr. Miller shrugged. "I don't get paid near enough anyway. I'd survive."

"Aren't you afraid the beast will come after you?" Fred asked.

"Nope," Skinny said. "The beast won't bother me."

"Why not?" I asked.

"Because unlike you kids, I know how to keep my nose out of places where it doesn't belong!" Skinny replied.

Fred and I left Skinny's campsite and walked back to our camp. Velma, Shaggy and Scooby were there waiting for us.

We all exchanged stories. Velma told us about the meeting with Mr. Richardson, and the sapphire they found in the woods. Fred told them about the book of gem dealers that Skinny had.

"Are you thinking what I'm thinking?" Velma asked.

Fred nodded.

"It's time to set a trap for the Bigfoot Beast!"

Fred and Daphne's Mystery-Solving Tips

"Daphne and I found an important clue in this entry. Make sure you answer all of the questions about it."

1. What clue did you find in this entry?

2. Who does the clue belong to?

3. How does this clue connect to the clue Velma found in the last entry?

Clue Keeper Entry 8

It didn't take the gang and I long to come up with a plan. To make it work, we needed Shaggy and Scooby to lure the Bigfoot Beast out of the woods.

Fred handed Shaggy his fishing pole.

"Like, do you expect us to fish for the monster?" Shaggy asked. "We're looking for the Bigfoot Beast, not the Bigfinned Flounder."

"We need to find an excuse for you and Scooby to go near the stream," Velma said. "If my hunch is right, the beast won't want you to go anywhere near there."

"Right," Fred said. He held up a fishing net. "When the beast comes after you, we'll be hiding in the trees with Mr. Walden. We'll trap the beast in this."

"What do you mean, when the beast comes after us?" Shaggy said. "What if it gets us and eats us for supper?"

Scooby didn't like that idea. He crawled into Velma's sleeping bag.

"Come on out, Scooby," I said. "We'll be right there to protect you."

"*Ruh-uh*," Scooby said.

"Would you do it for a Scooby Snack?" I asked.

"*Ruh-uh*," Scooby said.

"How about three Scooby Snacks," Daphne said, "and a big stack of pancakes when this trip is over?"

"*Rokay!*" Scooby said. He popped his head out of the sleeping bag.

It didn't take us long to set up the trap. Luckily, the woods were deserted. We didn't see Skinny Miller or Mindy Podwick anywhere.

Shaggy and Scooby-Doo sat down on the stream bank. Shaggy cast the fishing line into the water.

"Like, Scoob and I are sure having fun fishing in this stream," Shaggy said in a loud voice. He reeled in the line. "Hey, look, I caught something."

Sticking onto the end of the hook was a hunk of sparkling blue stone.

"Wow! Look at this!" Shaggy cried. "It's just like the one Velma found this morning."

"*Aaaaaaargh!*"

"Gee, Scoob," Shaggy said. "You sure sound excited."

Shaggy turned and looked at Scooby. But Scooby wasn't saying anything. Scooby had his back turned to the stream. He was pointing in front of him with a terrified look on his face.

Shaggy turned around. The Bigfoot Beast was standing right over them.

"*Aaaaargh!*" the beast roared. His beady red eyes glared at Shaggy and Scooby. He stomped his big, hairy feet.

"Let's get outta here, Scoob!" Shaggy yelled, dropping the fishing pole. They both stood up, but the ground underneath their feet was soft and slippery. With a splash, they both fell into the stream.

The Bigfoot Beast followed them into the stream. Shaggy and Scooby ran out, covered with water and mud. They tripped over their feet as they ran, falling into a pile of leaves.

Shaggy and Scooby ran into the woods. The Bigfoot Beast wasn't far behind.

Then suddenly, a net fell over Shaggy and Scooby.

"Gotcha!" a voice cried.

Fred and Mr. Walden jumped out from

behind a tree. Fred's face fell when he saw who was in the net.

"Shaggy and Scooby!" Fred said. "We thought you were the Bigfoot Beast! The mud and leaves make you look like a monster."

"Never mind that now," I said. "The real beast is getting away!"

The Bigfoot Beast was running down the trail, toward the cave near Skinny Miller's campsite.

"Don't worry," Velma said. She came running through the woods carrying the fishing pole.

Velma cast the fishing line. The line flew

through the air, and the hook caught in the Bigfoot Beast's fur. The beast stopped in his tracks.

Fred and I ran up to help Velma. Together, we reeled in the beast.

The creature roared as he was dragged backward along the trail. Shaggy and Scooby untangled themselves from the net. Mr. Walden joined the gang and me, and soon we had the Bigfoot Beast surrounded.

"Like, there's something fishy about this beast," Shaggy said.

"You can say that again," Velma said. She turned to Mr. Walden. "Would you like to see who's been trying to scare people away from your campground?"

"You bet I would!" Mr. Walden said. He grabbed a fistful of the Bigfoot Beast's hair and pulled off his fake head.

"**M**ore pancakes, please," Shaggy calls to the waitress.

You look up from reading the gang's Clue Keeper.

"That was quite a case, wasn't it?" Daphne says. "You've met the suspects. You've found the clues. Do you want to try to solve the mystery?"

You nod your head.

"I knew you could do it," Velma said. "Let us give you some advice before you start. Look at your list of suspects and clues and answer these questions."

"First, who had a reason to scare people away from the campground?" Fred asks.

"Second, which of the suspects could have left the clues that the Bigfoot Beast left?" Daphne asks.

"See if you can eliminate any of the suspects first," Velma says. "Whoever is left is probably the person pretending to be the Bigfoot Beast."

The waitress brings two new stacks of pancakes to the table. The stacks are so high that they cover Shaggy's and Scooby's faces.

"Why don't you try to solve the mystery while Scooby and Shaggy work on those pancakes?" Velma says.

"That won't take long!" Shaggy says.

"When you're done, we'll tell you who did it," Fred says.

"Zoinks! It's your last chance to guess who's behind the Bigfoot scare. When you're ready with your answer, turn the page to find out who did it!"

"It was Skinny Miller, the caretaker," Fred says.

"Our first clue was the footprints," Daphne says. "The fact that they were small meant that we were dealing with a real person in a costume, not a monster with giant feet."

"Mr. Richardson's feet were too big," Velma says. "And I believed Mindy Podwick when she said she wouldn't trample her fossils. She cared about them too much."

"That left Skinny Miller," Fred says.

"That left the question — why?" Velma

says. "We knew Skinny complained about not having any money. But closing the campground wouldn't help him."

"We started to figure it out when Velma found that sapphire," Daphne says. "Then I noticed something sparkling in the stream bed near Skinny's campsite. And we found Skinny's book of gem dealers."

"We knew that Skinny knew something about gems and jewels," Velma adds. "He told us his family used to be in the jewelry business. And he said the Bigfoot Beast's eyes looked like rubies."

"We figured that Skinny had discovered the sapphires in the stream bed," Fred says. "Instead of going to Mr. Walden, he decided to scare people away from the camp. That way he could harvest the sapphires, sell them, and keep the money for himself."

"They really belong to Mr. Walden," Velma explains. "He's going to use the money to keep the campground going. He's "Like, how about we camp out in this diner?" Shaggy suggests. "No trees. Lots of good food. And no monsters! Right, Scoob?"

even going to help Mindy Podwick study the fossils in peace."

"Mr. Walden's really a happy camper now, right, Scoob?" Shaggy asks.

Scooby gulps down the last pancake. "*Right!*"

Fred turns to you. "So, how did you do?" Fred asks.

"I bet you did great!" Daphne says. "And don't worry if you didn't. Solving mysteries can be pretty challenging. That's why it takes all of us working together to solve our mysteries."

Scooby-Doo nods his head. "*Roooby-Rooby-Roo!*"